SHORT TALES CLASSICS

EDGAR RICE BURROUGHS'

TARZAN of the Apes

The Man-Child

Adapted and Illustrated by
Shannon Eric Denton

GREEN LEVEL
- Familiar topics
- Frequently used words
- Repeating language patterns

BLUE LEVEL
- New ideas introduced
- Larger vocabulary
- Variety of language patterns

PINK LEVEL
- More complex ideas
- Extended vocabulary
- Expanded sentence structures

To learn more about Short Tales leveling, go to www.abdopublishing.com

Published by Magic Wagon, a division of the ABDO Publishing Group, 8000 West 78th Street, Edina, Minnesota, 55439. Copyright © 2008 by Abdo Consulting Group, Inc. International copyrights reserved in all countries. All rights reserved. No part of this book may be reproduced in any form without written permission from the publisher. Short Tales ™ is a trademark and logo of Magic Wagon.

Printed in the United States.

Written by Edgar Rice Burroughs
Adapted text by Shannon Eric Denton
Illustrations by Shannon Eric Denton
Colors by Wes Hartman
Edited by Stephanie Hedlund
Interior Layout by Kristen Fitzner Denton
Book Design and Packaging by Shannon Eric Denton

Library of Congress Cataloging-in-Publication Data
Denton, Shannon Eric.
  Edgar Rice Burroughs' Tarzan of the apes : the man-child / adapted and illustrated by Shannon Eric Denton.
    p. cm. -- (Short tales classics)
  ISBN 978-1-60270-123-6
  [1. Feral children--Fiction. 2. Apes--Fiction.] I. Burroughs, Edgar Rice, 1875-1950. Tarzan of the apes. II. Title. III. Title: Tarzan of the apes. IV. Title: Man-child.
PZ7.D4373Ed 2008
[Fic]--dc22
                                    2007036972

Contents

CHAPTER ONE: STRANDED

John Clayton, known as Lord Greystoke, and his wife, Alice, were stranded!

The jungle was to be their new home.

John and Alice had a baby on the way.   They needed a
sturdy place to live.

The house needed to be strong enough to protect them
from the elements.

It would also have to keep out the beasts that lived in
the jungle.

John got to work building a cabin.

After a month of solid work, John had built a fine shelter for his family.

At night, they could hear beasts prowling the jungle. The sounds made them nervous.

Time slowly passed.

Eventually, John built an addition to their small cabin.

Alice was growing used to their new life and the adventure that came with it.

However, one night Alice awoke believing it was all a dream.

John comforted his wife.

Reassured, Alice went back to sleep.

That night Alice gave birth to their son.

Despite being stranded, Alice and John were truly happy.
They had a beautiful child.

Their son would grow up without fear of his jungle
surroundings.

CHAPTER TWO: STARTING OVER

Changes happen quickly in the jungle.

One year later, young Greystoke's life changed forever.
After several attacks by apes, John and Alice died.

Their orphan son was adopted by a kind ape named Kala.

She would care for him now that there was no one else to do so.

The other apes were curious about this hairless child.

Kala was very protective and snarled at all who came near.

The other apes soon learned to approach Kala carefully.

She only let a few apes look at the child.

Kala took very good care of young Lord Greystoke.

She fed him.

She cleaned him.

She protected him.

Kala did this for a long time.

She began to love the man-child.

Kala never let him out of her sight.

Every day was much the same.

Kala hoped that he would soon begin to care for himself.

Despite her hopes, the child did nothing different.

The man-child grew as time passed.

But, he grew slowly.

Kala was a little worried about him.

Unlike the other children, he wasn't swinging from trees or climbing them.

In fact, he was just learning to walk.

And, she had been with him for a year now!

CHAPTER THREE: HE IS MINE

This may have upset other parents but not Kala.

Even if the child was slow, she cared deeply for him.

Her husband, Tublat, felt sorry for the human child.

After all, the rest of the children were much more advanced.

Kala did not care. She knew her child was special.

She couldn't have loved him any more than she already did.

The other apes noticed how different he was.

They noticed it when they traveled in a large group.

Other ape children held onto their mother as they moved through the jungle.

Kala had to hold little Greystoke when they traveled.

Many of the other apes stared, but Kala didn't care.

Her man-child was slow, but he was starting to learn.

He could eat a banana. He could make sounds.

Kala was very proud.

Young Greystoke often stared at the apes, too.

He was interested in them. They were big.

They were furry. He was not.

CHAPTER FOUR: WHITE SKIN

Young Greystoke always stared at the biggest, furriest ape.

This ape was Kerchack.

He was the leader, the king ape.

And, he was huge.

None of the other apes made eye contact with Kerchack.

They feared him.

They would look away if Kerchack looked at them.

Young Greystoke did not.

The man-child's stare angered mighty Kerchack.

Young Greystoke was lucky Kala protected him.

Kerchack wasn't afraid of Kala.

But, he didn't want to make her angry either.

So, Kerchack tried to scare the man-child into looking away.

His stare could make anyone turn away.

But young Greystoke kept looking at him.

Finally, the mighty Kerchak looked away.

Often, the apes spent their days in a clearing in the jungle.

The older apes rested and cleaned themselves.

The children played.

Young Greystoke tried to keep up with them.

He fell several times.

Every time he did, Kala was there to help him up.

She was never more than an arm's length away.

As the days passed, young Greystoke became tougher.

He could run now.

He still couldn't run very well, but it was an improvement.

30

But, he still couldn't climb.

Kala loved the child. She named him Tarzan, the
White Ape.

And in return, Tarzan loved his mother.